The Lion and the Mouse

with

The Donkey and the Lapdog

Illustrated by Val Biro

Award Publications Limited

One day a hungry lion caught a little mouse. The lion wanted to eat him up.

"I am too small to fill your belly," said the mouse. "Please let me go, and I promise to help you one day."

The lion laughed. "How could a tiny mouse ever help me?" But he let the mouse go because he had been so brave.

Soon after that, the lion was walking in the forest when he was caught in a hunter's net. He roared with anger.

All the animals were scared of
the lion and they ran away.

But when the mouse heard
the roar he knew the lion must
be in trouble. He ran to help.

The lion watched in surprise
as the mouse nibbled through
the ropes of the net.

The lion was free!
"Thank you, little friend!" smiled the lion. "I was wrong to think a mouse could not help a lion."

The Donkey and
the Lapdog

There was once a
farmer who worked hard.
He lived happily with his wife
in their cosy farmhouse.

They kept two animals, a big grey donkey and a small brown lapdog.

KK501270

From sunrise to sunset, the donkey worked hard pulling the cart on the farm.

At night, the donkey slept in the stable. But he kept thinking about the lapdog.

While the donkey was working in the fields all day, the lapdog played games in the house.

At night, while the donkey slept outside, the lapdog had a soft, warm bed indoors.

The donkey ate his food in
the barn, while the lapdog sat
on the farmer's lap to eat.

The donkey was very
jealous. "Perhaps the farmer
would like me better if I was
like the lapdog," he thought.

So he trotted into the house
and played like the lapdog did.
"Now the farmer will like me."

But the clumsy donkey kicked over the table, spilling the food and breaking the plates.

Then he jumped up onto the farmer's knee, just as he had seen the lapdog do.

But the farmer did not fuss over him. He only shouted and pushed the poor donkey away.

The farmer, his wife and the
lapdog all chased the donkey
back to his stable.

"How silly of me to pretend to be a lapdog," the donkey thought as he ran to his stable.

"I was foolish to try to be something I am not. From now on I shall just be myself."
And he has done just that.